P9-DDM-182

APR 2014
CH

White Socks Only

Evelyn Coleman

Illustrations by
Tyrone Geter

ALBERT WHITMAN & COMPANY
Chicago, Illinois

CH

Also by Evelyn Coleman:

To Be a Drum

The Riches of Oseola McCarty

Library of Congress Cataloging-in-Publication Data

Coleman, Evelyn, 1948-
White socks only / written by Evelyn Coleman; illustrated by Tyrone Geter.
p. cm.
Summary: Grandma tells the story about her first trip alone into town
during the days when segregation still existed in Mississippi.
ISBN 10: 0-8075-8956-X
ISBN 13: 978-0-8075-8956-4
[1. Afro-Americans—Fiction. 2. Race Relations—Fiction. 3. Mississippi—Fiction.] I. Geter, Tyone, ill.
II. Title.
PZ7.C6746Wh 1996 95-38324 [Fic]—dc20 CIP AC

The text typeface is Stone Informal.
The illustrations are rendered in alkyds and oil paint.
The design is by Susan B. Cohn.

For more information about Albert Whitman & Company,
visit our web site at www.albertwhitman.com

To my brother, Edward (Eddie Joe) Coleman, who
believed in the magic of my stories. E.C.

To the children of the world. You are the future. T.G.

G randma, can I walk into town by myself?" I asked, one hot summer's day. I knew what she was going to say. She was going to tell a story. Not just any story, but my favorite story.

I watched her turn toward her spit can. Ping! The snuff juice hit the bottom, sounding like a chime. She rocked one or two times, her eyes closed, and then she looked up at me.

"You know you ain't big enough to walk into no town alone, girl. I sho' don't know why you asking me that. You ain't big enough 'til you gon' do some good there."

I smiled and plopped down on the step. She was about to begin the story.

Grandma laughed.

You know. . . when I was a little girl, like yourself, I sneaked into town once. Yep, all by myself. Wasn't planning on doing no good. Had just been waiting for a scorching hot day. I had two eggs hid in my pockets. Not to eat, mind you. But to see if what folk said was true.

I slipped on my finest Sunday dress and my shiny black patent-leather shoes and my clean white socks. I pulled my plaits back with a bow. Why, I thought I looked pretty grown-up. Lord, you should a'seen me strutting, the dust flying behind me! I had to hold my arms steady on account of them eggs, though. Now that I think about it, I must'a been a mighty funny sight.

I sneaked on up that road a'singing, "Jump back Sally, Sally, Sally. Walking up the alley, alley, alley" to nobody but myself. And child, was it hot! On that kind of day a firecracker might light up by itself.

I was feeling pretty fine until I spotted that old Chicken Man, sitting on his porch, with his mouth like a smile. I just looked down at the dirt.

My mama had told me how the Chicken Man still did things he knowed all the way from Africa. Stuff that his grandmother done taught him. Mama also had told me he could heal the sick by the laying on of his hands. And that one time he made a blind man see just by looking deep into his eyes. And folk said he turned people into chickens if he didn't feel what they were doing was right. That's why he was called the Chicken Man.

I was kinda scared he might think I wasn't doing right, so I started walking faster. I still held my arms out steady, though, so I wouldn't break the eggs.

Anyway, when I got to town, I didn't see many folk that I knew. I wandered around, with my mouth gaped open, looking at the white women in their fancy hats. That's when I saw Mama's friend Miss Nancy turning the corner. I was going to sho nuff be in trouble if she saw me. She told Mama *everything.* So I took off running toward the first big tree I saw and hid behind it.

I stayed there for a minute, panting, until I saw Miss Nancy walk out of sight. Then I tiptoed out. But in my rush I'd burst one of my eggs, and it was slinking down my dress and legs.

I figured I'd better do what I come to do and get back home. I was standing in front of this big old building where there was a statue of a soldier sitting up on a horse. I read what it said on the building: "Cole County Courthouse, Mississippi."

I carefully pulled my egg out of my pocket. Right
there, I cracked it one time against the horse's leg.

The egg's insides dropped to the hot cement. I knelt down with my face close. I watched that egg like the old men watch the checkers before making a move. For a minute I thought it wasn't gon' do nothing.

Then right around the edges, I saw it. One little bit was turning white. Next the white creeped wider and the yellow began to bubble. By golly, I was frying an egg on the cement just like folk said!

I jumped up and started dancing and prancing.

It was time to go home now. I'd done it. It was all over, and it was true. It could get so hot you could fry an egg on the sidewalk.

I started walking and wiping sweat from my face, with the eggy part of my dress sticking to me every time I took a step. My mouth was dry as dirt, and I was mighty thirsty. That's when I spotted the water fountain. It had a little stepstool so children could climb up to drink. But on the fountain was a sign that read, "Whites Only."

Well, I knew what *that* meant. So I sat down in the grass and took off my shiny black patent-leather shoes. Now I only had on my clean white socks. I stepped up on that stool with those white socks hugging my feet.

I was slurping up that water mighty fast when this big white man with a black and white bandanna 'round his neck grabbed me off the stool and pushed me to the ground. The white man pointed to the sign and yelled at me, "Can't you read, girl? Why, I'm gon' whup you 'til you can't sit down." His big fingers fumbled and tugged at his belt.

I began to cry as a crowd of white people gathered 'round. They were all staring at me. Seeing all the people made me real scared, and I cried louder. I couldn't understand what the white man was so mad about. I was wearing my white socks.

An old black woman from my church stepped through the crowd. She wasn't wearing anything white, but she untied her shoes and took them off. She stepped up to the fountain, bent way down, and took a drink.

I knew the man was gon' yell at her. And he did. "I'm gon' have to whup you too, ain't I?" he shouted.

But then other black folk started coming over,
removing their shoes and drinking from the fountain.
They had on clean-looking green socks and yellow socks
and red socks and blue socks.

Of course, the big man with the bandanna kept right
on yelling. His face got red as fire. He was snorting
through his nose like a bull does when it's gon' charge.

Other white folk came up and started yelling at us, too. By that time, the big man had whipped his belt out of his pants. He was hitting me and everybody else who was close. None of the black people moved. They just covered their faces. I sat there sobbing, holdin' my arms over my head.

All of a sudden everybody got quiet like they was gon' pray in church. Even the white people. I peeped out through my arms. The black people and the white people were moving aside. The Chicken Man was coming through. He was slowly tapping his way toward me.

When he got close, he stopped. He looked at me from the top of my head down to my white socks. Then he bent over and pulled off his black shoes, his face squeezing up. He had on the cleanest white socks you ever seen.

He stepped up on the stool. He didn't have to bend over very far because he was so short. He drank a long time from that fountain.

I held my breath. So did everyone else.

The Chicken Man lifted his head. He turned around, smiling, and slowly stepped down off the stool. Without a word, he pointed a crooked finger at the white man. The white man's belt was down by his side now, clasped tightly in his fist. He was as still as the statue.

The old Chicken Man helped me up. He took out a white handkerchief and wiped off my face. "There, there now, child. It's time for you to go on home. You did all right." He handed me a chicken feather out of the brim of his hat and hobbled away.

All the black people surrounded me. They were all crying and hugging me. Then they took me home.

When they told Mama what had happened, she just broke out laughing. She said, "Well I guess you can go to town by yourself now 'cause you're old enough to do some good."

Nobody ever again saw the big white man who had whipped us. None of us dared ask about the big chicken flapping 'round the courthouse near the water fountain, neither.

And from then on, the "Whites Only" sign was gone from that water fountain forever.